DISCARD

A WOODPECKER'S TALE

Published in Canada by Fitzhenry & Whiteside, 195 Allstate Parkway, Markham, ON, L3R 4T8
www.fitzhenry.ca
Published in the U.S. by Fitzhenry & Whiteside, 311 Washington Street, Brighton, Massachusetts 02135

We acknowledge with thanks the Canada Council for the Arts, and the Ontario Arts Council for their support of our publishing program. We acknowledge the financial support of the Government of Canada through the Canada Book Fund (CBF) for our publishing activities.

Library and Archives Canada Cataloguing in Publication
Cassidy, Sean, 1947-, author, illustrator
A woodpecker's tale / Sean Cassidy.
ISBN 978-1-55455-284-9 (bound)
I. Title.
PS8555.A78122W66 2014   jC813.6   C2014-901003-6

Publisher Cataloging-in-Publication Data (U.S.)
Cassidy, Sean.
Woodpecker's tale / Sean Cassidy.
[32] pages : cm.
Summary: "A young woodpecker decides he is old enough to venture out and hunt for insects on his own. But when he sets out to prove to his mother that he is old enough to be independent and responsible, he discovers that finding juicy insects isn't as easy as he'd thought it would be. The young woodpecker has to figure out a way to get what he wants in this coming-of-age story."
ISBN-13: 978-1-55455-284-9
1. Woodpeckers – Juvenile fiction. I. Title.
[E] dc23 PZ7.C3884Wo   2014

Text and cover design by Daniel Choi
Cover illustration courtesy of Sean Cassidy

Printed and bound in China by Sheck Wah Tong Printing Press Ltd.

A WOODPECKER'S TALE

SEAN CASSIDY

Fitzhenry & Whiteside

For Maggie,
who flies so beautifully

Pierce knew that he was old enough to leave the nest.

"But you're so young," Mama fretted.
"Who will feed you?"

"I will feed myself," piped Pierce.

"But you don't know where to find
your food."

Pierce puffed out his chest. "I've watched you, Mama.
Find an old tree. Hammer the wood.
Eat the yummy bugs.
I can do it."

"But some bugs are nasty.
They can hurt," called Mama
as Pierce scampered off.
"Be careful!"

Pierce landed on a hollow trunk
that had fallen
many summers before
he poked out of his shell.

"I can almost smell the bugs inside," he chirped.

He hammered his beak into the spongy wood.

He tossed aside a cluster of splinters and spotted
a juicy bug.

As Pierce tried to spear it with his tongue, Skunk snapped,
"Stop hammering holes in my roof."

She turned her back and raised her tail.

Pierce dashed for shelter.

Stinking drops of skunk oil splashed around him.

The stench nettled his nose.

Pierce wove through the forest muttering, "That was close.
I'll find an old tree that is still standing."

He circled an ancient trunk
that had lost its branches.
Landing near the top,
he hammered the wood.

When he leaned back to hammer again,

Pierce saw two eyes,

each one almost as large as his head,

glaring down at him.

"WHO are YOU?" snapped Owl.

"YOU just WOKE me."

Spooked, Pierce leaped back and tumbled down and away.

His feathers trembled.
His tummy growled.
He wobbled among the trees
searching for food.

"Finding food is scary,"
he mumbled as he spied
an old beech tree.

"It looks like
nobody lives here," he chirped,
circling the tree.

"My babies live here," snarled Raccoon.

Pierce jumped away again.

He fluttered across a meadow
and flopped onto the base
of a tree to rest.
As he lay panting,
the feathers on his back
prickled like they did when
danger was near.

Pierce whirled around and shrieked. Opossum, surprised, shrieked, too.

Pierce bolted.

Opossum played dead.

"I'll never find anything as good as the log

that Skunk won't let me near," he grumbled.

He heard a humming sound, a hum

that could only be made by bugs—lots of bugs.

They buzzed in and out of a hole

in a nearby oak.

Pierce chuckled.

It was a nest of tasty bugs.

He poked the nest. A few bees buzzed angrily.

"Oh, a nest of **nasty** bugs."
He pondered the bugs.
"Nasty bugs may be just what I need."

He took a shuddering breath
and jabbed the nest again as hard as he could.
Furious bees surged forward.

Pierce sprang away and sped toward home.

"Bees!" he shrieked as he flapped past Opossum.

Pierce zoomed back
across the meadow
and among the trees.

"Bees!" he squealed
as he hovered near
Raccoon.

He flew past Owl, screaming, "Bees! Nasty bees!"

Owl ducked into his twiggy nest.

Pierce puffed. His throat ached.
He forced his wings to flap
as he zigzagged through the woods.

Nearing Skunk's log, he darted through the open end.

"Bees!" he shrieked.

"Bees?" gasped Skunk.
She dashed out
the other end
of the log.

The bees blasted
after her.

Pierce flopped against the outside of the log
and watched them disappear into the woods.

Pierce plunged his beak into the spongy log.

Something tickled his tongue.

He speared it and feasted on a juicy bug.

Pierce ate until his tummy was full.

He flew home to rest.

Pierce closed his eyes and chuckled.

"I knew it would be easy."

FIND THE WOODPECKERS

There are thirteen silhouettes of a standing woodpecker hidden in the pictures. How many can you find?

BONUS: Find the silhouette of a flying bird.

WOOD TOOLS CHECKLIST

If you wanted to dig a hole into the side of a tree, you would need special tools, like sharp chisels and a hammer. Woodpeckers have their own special tools for working with wood.

- ✔ Hard and very pointy beaks for digging into wood
- ✔ Special padding around their brains to prevent headaches
- ✔ Strong toes to grip the bark on the side of a tree
- ✔ Stiff tail feathers that dig into the bark for extra support
- ✔ A good sense of smell to find insects
- ✔ Feathers that protect their nostrils from wood chips
- ✔ Long, pointy, barbed tongues to find and spear insects under the bark

WOODPECKER WORLD

There are about 200 different kinds of woodpeckers. They live almost everywhere there are trees, except in Australia and some islands, like New Zealand and Madagascar.

The easiest way to find a woodpecker is to go to a place with lots of trees, especially old trees with dead branches. Listen for the tat-tat-tat drumming sound that the woodpecker makes when tapping a tree with its beak. The springtime is the best time for this, because that is when woodpeckers make lots of noise attracting mates and hollowing out their nests.

HOW TO FIND INSECTS IN A TREE

When insects bore into wood, they create hollow areas and tunnels. Woodpeckers find these hollow spots by tapping with their beaks, and listening to the sound of the tapping.

Try It Yourself

Although woodpeckers tap with their beaks, you can find hollow spots in wood by tapping with a different tool.

Use a chopstick, a pen with the point covered, a pencil without an eraser, a thin paint brush, or any short hard stick.

Get permission to **gently** tap on something made of wood. The top of a desk is ideal.

Tap in the middle of the desk top where it is hollow underneath. Listen to how the sound changes as you tap gently while moving toward an edge of the desk, where there is a solid support beneath the top.

When searching for food, woodpeckers will spiral up a tree trunk, tapping and listening for hollows that insects have made under the bark. Their long tongues slide into the hollows and remove the insects.

FROM EGG TO ADULT

Keep Eggs Warm

Most female woodpeckers will lay four or five small white eggs. Both parents take turns keeping the eggs warm by resting on them. The eggs hatch in about twelve days on average.

Leave the Nest

At the end of this time, the nestlings are almost as big as their parents! The nest is getting crowded. The nestlings take turns sitting in the entrance hole and watching the world outside. When the nestlings reach this stage, they are big enough to leave the nest and start flying.

The tired parents stop bringing food. One hungry nestling hops out of the nest onto a branch and calls for food. When the parents still don't bring any, it spreads its wings and takes a short flight to a nearby tree, where it hides among the leaves. One by one, the other nestlings do the same.

APRIL	MAY	JUNE

Feed the Nestlings

For the next two and a half weeks, both parents bring food to the nestlings. In one day, each parent could make between 125 and 150 trips to the nest with food. The parents feed the nestlings, every three minutes, for the next seventeen or eighteen days. That adds up to about 5000 feedings.

Young Grow and Learn

The parents start feeding the young again for the next couple of days. During this time, the parents show the young woodpeckers how to find their own food.

HOW TO DRAW A WOODPECKER

Draw an egg that is leaning to one side.

Draw a circle for the head.

Draw the beak.

Draw the wing.

Draw the foot.

Add another foot behind the first foot.

Add feathers along the body and erase some lines.

Have fun with crayons or paint.

VIRGINIA OPOSSUM

An opossum is a marsupial—a mammal that has a pouch to carry its babies—and it's the only marsupial that exists in North America. In general, when most animals feel threatened, they either run away, or they act like they want to fight the animal or the person threatening them. Opossums are unique in that when they feel threatened, they fall sideways and pretend that they are dead. This is called *playing possum*. They can play possum for several hours. When they do this, most other animals simply leave them alone.

QUIZ: WHAT KIND OF WOODPECKER ARE YOU?

Which of these best describes you?

1. I like tapping on old, spongy trees and finding tasty treats inside.
2. Drilling holes into trees and licking up the yummy sap inside is the best!
3. I prefer to hunt on the ground for scrumptious ants.

If you chose...

1) You're a ***common woodpecker***. Most woodpeckers live in trees and find most of their insects and beetles in trees.

2) You're a ***sapsucker***. These are woodpeckers that drill a series of small holes in the bark of a tree and sip the tree's sap as it fills the holes. Other birds and small animals, like squirrels, also visit these holes for a bit of sap.

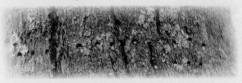

3) You're a ***flicker***. These are woodpeckers that feed on the ground. They flick leaves and twigs aside to get at the ants beneath. A woodpecker's tongue is very long—at least twice the length of its beak. A flicker's tongue is about 12 cm (5 inches) long. It is smoother than other woodpecker tongues, but very sticky for catching ants.